Spiritual Genetics

The DNA of God

By

T.C. Chiles Sr.

For the family family father

Copyright © 2003 by T.C. Chiles Sr.

Spiritual Genetics
by T.C. Chiles Sr.

Printed in the United States of America

Library of Congress Control Number: 2003104788
ISBN 1-591607-55-8

Unless otherwise indicated, Bible quotations are taken from the King James Version of the Bible. Copyright © 1963 by Finis Jennings Dake.

Xulon Press
www.XulonPress.com

Xulon Press books are available in bookstores everywhere, and on the Web at www.XulonPress.com.

Foreword

The study of **Genetics** has come a tremendous distance in the last few decades. We now understand the process of DNA and genetic makeup, genetic encoding and so forth. In today's technological discussion of genetics, there are many terms and phrases that are used. You may or may not be familiar with some or all of these terms. One of these is DNA. DNA is defined as "the chemical substance that transfers genetic characteristics. DNA transfers the characteristics of the original to its offspring. I believe that God's Spirit is HIS DNA.

Also you may have heard the term **genetic**. Well **genetic** simply means "of the origin, or origin of something". **Genetics** is that branch of biology that deals with heredity and variation in similar or related animals and plants. **Genetic code** is "the order in which chemical constituents are arranged in DNA molecules for transmitting genetic information to the cells."

I also believe that all things are parallel. The natural and then the spiritual. Natural knowledge here in the earth realm is parallel to already present spiritual knowledge in the spiritual realm. Everything here in the earth is a replica of a pattern of something in God's eternal Kingdom. (Ecc. 3:11, 15), (Matt. 6:10).

Just as natural knowledge has increased concerning the study of genetics and in particular the study of DNA, I believe we are also receiving spiritual revelation knowledge concerning Kingdom truths and principles, Kingdom science and Kingdom technology.

The Bible never declares that we the people of the Most High God are destroyed because of the power of the devil. On the contrary, scripture states that the very gates of Hell would not and could not prevail against the Church of Jesus Christ

(Matt. 16:18). However, the Bible does say that we perish or we are destroyed for the lack of knowledge (Hosea 4:6). This is the knowledge of the truth. It is the truth that makes us free (John 8:32). The truth of divine revelation and the revealing of God's will and purpose for mankind. It even goes on to tell us in Hosea 4 that not only will **we** suffer if **we** reject knowledge but also our **children** and **children's children.**

The enemy of our souls does not want us to really **know** and **believe** the complete will of God for our lives. But this is an exciting time for the Body of Christ. We are experiencing a restoration of Apostolic authority and divine government throughout the Church. The five-fold ministry gifts are being energized by this newest surge of Holy Ghost power and revelation knowledge. I'm also convinced that there is an emergence of a Davidic type people. A people of multiple anointings. Worshipers. Warriors. Priests. Kings. Prophets. Restorers. A people who **know** and understand their God and do exploits.

The nations and kingdoms of this world can only be won to Christ in this hour by a Church that has been infused with the very life and light of God. The very **DNA (Divine Nature Ability)** of the Most High God. Only this kind of blood-bought, spirit empowered, supernatural body of believers will prevail over the spiritual wickedness in high places. For this cause I submit to you what I believe to be a spiritual truth for such a time as this.

I also believe that the Church of Jesus Christ is on the brink of the greatest restoration of the healing gifts and sign and wonders that it has ever experienced since the early Church period. These miraculous works will accelerate an exciting harvest of souls (Isa. 45:8). Miracles will be the norm. The blind eye will be opened... The lame will walk... The leper will be cleansed... The dead shall be raised and the poor shall have the Gospel preached unto them.

Contents

Chapter 1

In the Beginning

(The DNA = Divine Nature Ability of the Father)

In the beginning God created the heavens and the earth (Gen 1). And then in Genesis 2:7 we read how God CREATED (Hebrew "bara" – to bring into being), MAN. Man is and was God's greatest creative achievement upon earth and he was made in God's image and likeness. The Bible teaches that Man is fearfully and wonderfully made (Ps. 139:14).

When God made man He first formed a body out of the chemical elements and substances found upon this planet. Then He breathed the breath (Hebrew "neshamah – puff or breath) of **life** (Hebrew "chayim – of lives) into his body. God the Father himself breathed the first "breath of life" into Adams nostrils. God breathed into this body made up of the elements of the earth some of **His** own **spiritual life, (DNA)**, and that life was contained in the substance we call blood. Blood is **not** life, but the blood carries life. The life of the living creature is **in** the blood. "For the life of the flesh is in the **blood**", (Lev. 17:11).

After God breathed into Adam, he became a "living soul" (Gen. 2). God had given Adam a blood infusion. Adam had been given the very **DNA** of God the Father. This life of God, or DNA of God the Father, is carried in our bloodstream. The life itself is **spiritual**, but it must have a physical carrier and that substance is our blood.

How awesome and amazing is this substance called blood. A drop of blood the size of a **pinhead** is packed with **five million** red blood cells. These cells carry oxygen, that they pick up in the lungs, **ninety thousand** miles roundtrip throughout the blood vessels and heart and then return to the lungs and expel the carbon dioxide. Then there are white blood cells. There is one white cell for every one thousand red cells. They are the warriors/defenders/cleansers of this **temple-kingdom** we call the BODY. Their task is to protect the body against invading impurities and keep it rejuvenated that it may function properly for hundreds of years. (In actuality our bodies were originally made to be eternal, breathing in oxygen, taking in nutriment orally and being self-perpetuating. Never to run down or needing to recharge the battery.) All of this was set into motion when God injected His **DNA** into the man Adam. Within that **DNA** was the **Code for Life.**

The most amazing thing about our blood is its capacity to carry the life of God. The connection between the Divine and the human rests in the blood stream. Blood indeed is a mysterious substance. It contains what no scientist can explain…it contains the very **life, DNA, of God!** How awesome is Father God. He had now created inhabitants here on the planet earth that had His very DNA and Life in them. His blood. His divine energy and light.

Adam and Eve before the fall had the very life and DNA of God the Father flowing through their veins. They were destined to rule over the earth and take dominion over all of

God's creation (Gen 1 & 2). They had God's DNA (Divine Nature Ability) and the ability to live just as God lives. Eternal blood equals life. They were to live in His image and likeness. They were to be fruitful and multiply and replenish the earth. What a glorious state for man to be in. They had the full use of their brain, intellect and spirit. The Bible says that Father God gave Adam the assignment to name every living thing that was upon the earth and he did (Gen 2:19-20). How awesome and marvelous was this man created in the image of God and containing the very DNA of God in his life. Nothing would be impossible for him.

Chapter 2

God's Genetic Engineering

In Genesis chapter 3, we read the details of how Adam and Eve sinned against Father God and lost their Divine birthright. There was a transgression of the Law of God. They allowed the elements of the kingdom of darkness to enter in through their rebellion against the kingdom of light. The **pure** bloodline had now become tainted. Rebellion and disobedience had brought about contamination. Spiritual adultery had caused a breach in the genetic code. No longer was there a Divine genetic ability within Adam. No longer would he and his wife live eternally like God. No longer would he be able to walk in Divine health and prosperity. Decay had set in. Destruction would be the ultimate end because the heavenly gene pool had become **dis-connect**. The DNA was contaminated ("con" – with; "taminat" – taint).

Now man began to experience the effects of an altered code of life. His spirit was introduced to fear immediately after the fall (Gen. 3:10). Sorrows were pronounced upon him in connection with the sex appetite (Gen. 3:16). Sorrows were pronounced upon him in connection with the food appetite (Gen. 3:17). Adam and Eve had never before experienced sorrow, fear, sickness, shame or a host of other things. They had to learn these foreign behaviors, emotions and conditions.

In the Garden before the fall, man had the availability of 100% of his brainpower. He could draw upon 100% of the ability programmed into him by his heavenly genetic code. After sin, contamination entered his environment. Man's spiritual genetic makeup was altered and deteriorated to where it is today. According to scientist, we only use half our brain and only 10% of that half. The human race was on a downhill journey into a bleak situation.

God had to give a remedy for this situation or man would live generation after generation in this degraded state and that was not why God had created him. He had created mankind that He might have sons and daughters made in His image to worship, to love and commune with Him (Gen 1:26-28, Rom. 8:29, Deut. 11:13).

That remedy, or prescription, would be a **blood transfusion**. Just as the natural life is in the blood, the spiritual life is in the blood also. Man needed a spiritual blood transfusion that would bring him back to that place with God of the original creation. God had to once again introduce His blood and His DNA (Divine Nature Ability) into the human race. His creation needed to be redeemed.

The only element that could blot out the spiritual wickedness committed buy *by* Adam and Eve was blood (I Pet. 1:18-19, Rev. 5:9b, Titus 2:14, Eph. 1:7, Col. 1:14). Nothing could atone for their sin but blood (Heb. 9:22, I John 5:6, I John 1:7). Nothing could redeem mankind from the penalty of their treason but blood. The only thing that could ever restore mankind back to eternal life was blood. Life for life...blood for blood (Gen. 9:6, Gen. 3:22).

God had to once again take some of His life, or His DNA, or His blood, or His breath and place it into a body made from the substances of this earth. He would then have to take that body with His DNA or blood within it and shed it for all mankind to partake of by faith.

The prescription was written before man was even ejected from the Garden. Father God began to lay out His purpose and plan to reconcile man back to Himself through a blood sacrifice. Father God allowed one of the animals to be killed to provide a covering for the shame and nakedness of Adam and Eve. An innocent life was taken and its blood shed and its skin used to cover man's iniquity. As long as Adam and Eve lived, they now had to shed innocent blood of the animals that perhaps Adam himself had named, to provide a covering for their rebellion against God's laws. This was but a type and shadow of what Father God would someday do Himself. Allowing Jesus, the Lamb of God to be slain on the cross for the sins of the world (Gen 3:22, John 3:16, Rev. 5:12).

To bring about this marvelous plan of re-implanting His life and His DNA back into the human race, God the Father supernaturally prepared a body from the elements of this earth (Heb. 10:5), and placed that body in the form of a fetus into the womb of a virgin named Mary. Here was a new or second Adam. "Jesus, the last Adam..." (I Cor. 15:45). This body contained the life-blood or DNA of God himself. Not Mary and Joseph's blood but God the Father's blood. The Bible states that the Holy Spirit caused the conception of Jesus in the womb of Mary (Matt. 1:20).

Here was Jesus, the Son of God, taking on the form of a man and being sent supernaturally into the womb of Mary to be birthed into the earth realm. Taking on a body made from the elements of this world but without the contamination of Adam's sin. A body that lived by the pure, uncontaminated blood and DNA of Father God. Pure and Holy DNA. Pure and Holy blood. Divine blood that contained the Divine life of the Father of Lights.

Although Jesus was carried and formed and fashioned in the womb of Mary, it was the Life of God that flowed through His veins and that life emanated straight from the throne of God. He was the only begotten Son of God (John 1:14). The blood that He shed at Calvary was pure and uncontaminated. It was precious and priceless and without type. It was God's own blood being shed for mankind.

His blood was not contaminated with the Adamic sin which caused sin and sickness and the kingdom of darkness to enter into the DNA of God's creation. What a great price…redemption.

Adam and Eve had the opportunity to live without sin and keep the blood of the Father untainted in them. By their transgression they introduced death and destruction into the earth realm and the inhabitants thereof (Rom. 5:12). Now every human body born into the earth would become subject to corruption and decay and ultimately death. That's when the life of the body leaves the bloodstream with the soul and spirit.

By sending Jesus to the earth, God the Father resolved the sin issue with the ultimate sacrifice. Jesus lived a sinless life and there was no sin or contamination found in Him. The kingdom of darkness could not penetrate the light of God to taint and dilute the Divine substances within Him (The Holy Spirit). When Jesus allowed Himself to die for the sins of the world, He gave a perfect life filled with perfect blood to redeem mankind from the curse of imperfect blood filled with death and destruction. Life for life. Blood for blood (I Pet. 1:19).

What a wonderful picture of our salvation now unfolds. The instant that we believe on Jesus by faith and trust in what he accomplished on the cross and accept Him as Savior, a spiritual blood transfusion begins to take place. Sin that is within our bloodstreams naturally and spiritually begins to undergo a purging process (Joel 3:21). Cleansing begins in our hearts and then, eternal life...the Life of God...His DNA (Divine Nature Ability) and His Divine health become our portion.

God the Father had made it possible once again for mankind to draw from that Heavenly Gene pool and access the things of God as a partaker of his Divine nature and a member of the family of God (His Genos). There is power in the shed blood of Jesus to cleanse, remit, cover, etc. because His blood isn't from this earth. It is not carnal or of this world but it is mighty because it contains the DNA of God.

Chapter 3

Royal Bloodline

L et us move on further in our search for the truths of God concerning our position in Him and His position relative to us.

To be born again literally means to be "begotten from on high". If you are a Christian, you are a new species of being and you have inherited the very nature and Life of God the Father. His Spirit has come and imparted to you His very own Divine nature. You are a partaker of that Divine nature (II Pet. 1:4). You have inherited "eternal life" or the ZOE life. You have received the greatest miracle that can be performed on the earth. You have been given a new nature.

You have been recreated in spirit and are now of a new species. You have been born again of "incorruptible seed" (I Pet. 1:23). The old things have passed away and all things have become new (I Cor. 5:17). You are now a member of the **royal** family of God (John 15:5).

There are many terms available to describe what happens to a person when they believe on the Lord Jesus and accept Him as Savior. Some call it the New Birth. Others call it conversion. Still others say the born again experience. All of these terms are used to describe what takes place when a human being's spirit is taken out of the kingdom of darkness and translated over to the Kingdom of Light. This experience is a spiritual happening. The nature of Satan is replaced with the very life (ZOE) and DNA of God the Father that created all things. This experience restores one back into their original place with God as a son or daughter with all the rights and privileges of a member of the **royal** family.

Now we are no longer in the family of the devil but we are in the genos or family of God. We now have a new force that is leading us. His Nature. We are no longer driven by the forces of darkness, but we are now led by the Kingdom of light. Our bloodline has been changed. Our genetic encoding has been altered. It has been set aright. We have become priests and kings unto Him. Royalty. Our Father's nature flows into us. Our Father's nature flows out of us. The blood of Jesus has purchased our entrance back into the very throne room of the Most High God! We have received the very life and DNA (Divine Nature Access) of God by faith (Col. 1:13-14). We are His workmanship created in Christ Jesus (Eph. 2:10).

I John 3:2 declares "beloved, now are we the **sons** of God." We are a **royal** priesthood (I Pet. 2:9). We have His Divine life in us because we are His sons, begotten by Him from on high. Our bloodline is royal because of who we are. Sons and daughters of God. Demons recognize our royalty. Sickness and disease recognize our royalty. The forces of darkness recognize the authority that our Father the King has given unto us. God is in us by His Spirit (DNA). We are able to partake of His nature, His life and His very substance. We are His righteousness.

When the truth is revealed to us by the Holy Spirit (revelation) through the word concerning the fact that the very "ZOE" of God – the very life and nature of God the

Father resides in us (Col. 1:27) – sickness and dis-ease will have to flee. Any darkness will have to go! When we activate that revelation by mixing it with faith, we will see mighty, miraculous manifestations in our lives.

According to the Bible, Col. 1:13, we have been taken out of the kingdom of darkness and translated into the Kingdom of God's dear son Jesus.....by and through His blood! His DNA (Divine Nature Ability)! This Kingdom of God, or Kingdom of Heaven, is a Kingdom of light (Col. 1:13). When the light comes, the darkness has to go. It is a Kingdom of **Peace** and **Joy** in the Holy Ghost (Rom. 14:17). Sickness and dis-ease are from the kingdom of darkness (Satan's counterfeit kingdom). Poverty and lack are from the kingdom of darkness (Satan's realm). These things are not our inheritance as sons and daughters of God.

Whenever Jesus came into contact with sickness and disease, or the curse of sin and death, the life of God (DNA) within Him reacted by attempting to eradicate, or destroy, the works of the devil (I John 3:8). Jesus spoke from His own lips, "greater works shall ye do" (John 14:12). I believe that sometimes we don't see the "greater works" because we're not convinced ("con" – with; "vinced" –feeling) or convicted ("con" – with; "victed" – strong belief) that the "Greater One" is within us by His blood. His DNA (Divine Nature Ability).

Because of your spiritual bloodline, birthright and heritage, you can exert spiritual authority over the natural realm or earth realm. Just as the laws of physics and molecular structure were interrupted and altered by Peter as he walked on the water (Matt. 14:29)...just as those same laws were disrupted when the three Hebrew boys were thrown into the fiery furnace (Dan. 3:19-23)...just as Jesus turned the water into wine and multiplied the loaves and the fishes, so you also my friend possess the ability to command the laws of nature to obey when need be. Knowing this fact and putting it into practice will revolutionize your life in so many ways.

I'm convinced that for everything natural there is a spiritual parallel. Therefore all truth is parallel. Everything we know and perceive in this earthly realm existed first in the spiritual. Everything good in the natural is a pattern of the spiritual.

Sickness and dis-ease, lack and poverty are all learned behaviors that mankind took upon himself after the fall in the Garden of Eden. These things were not in his original encode or programming (DNA - ZOE life of God). Before the fall, (eating of the tree of the **Knowledge** of good and evil), man had no knowledge of sickness or lack. He lived continually at his **best** in the presence of God the Father who supplied his every need.

Now that we have been bought back into the royal family of God we have re-inherited the life and light of God through the will and testament of Jesus. Now we can partake of His Divine Nature. God's **DNA**. Divine Nature Access.....Divine Nature Ability.....and Divine Nature Attributes. Now, with this heavenly Genetic Code, we can access the supernatural power of God! If you have been born again, Father God has imbedded a spiritual "computer chip" in your inner man and in your mind (forehead) in the person of the Holy Ghost. Eph. 4:30, "And grieve not the Holy Spirit of God, whereby you are sealed unto the day of redemption."

We can and should partake of all the benefits that accompany our royal positioning in the family of God. His promises are real and no power in earth, under the earth or above the earth can stand against His elect.

Several years ago while conducting a healing crusade on the east coast, I had occasion to pray for a woman with a case of terminal cancer. As this fragile sister stood before me I began to pray in the spirit for God's direction. As I was praying the Lord began to reveal some things to me in my inner-man. Suddenly, I realized that this cancer was simply a group of cells within this body that had become "outlaw cells". Cells that were not functioning according to their pre-ordained purpose or blueprint. Cells that had come out from under God's Divine authority or government for that body. We are created in His image and likeness. Influenced by the kingdom of darkness, these cells had gone out of alignment. They had become mal-ignant. Mal-aligned. They were growing wildly and without order and were attempting a coup or takeover.

I quickly began to speak order into the chaotic situation just as the Father had done at the original creation (Gen. 1). I laid my hands on her (Mark 16:18) and commanded the cells and blood and the other organs to line up with the power and authority of God in Jesus' mighty name. Then I loosed the light and healing power of the almighty into that body and bound all of the "outlaw" cell activity and the "outlaw" spirit that was the author of the confusion, in the Name of Jesus. By faith I applied His stripes and His blood (DNA) to the situation. The sister was "miraculously" healed and is still healed to this day!

We have the God given right and God given ability to lay hands on the sick and see them recovered. As a matter of fact, we have the God given responsibility to do so. Why? First of all, because Jesus himself commanded us to do so (Mark 16:18). Secondly, because when we lay our hands on someone there is a "transmittal" that takes place. The life and DNA of God is so real and tangible that it can be imparted from one person to another. This is done through the person of God we call the Holy Spirit, the transmitter of that Life and Power (DNA). Eph. 3:20, "Now unto him that is able to do exceeding abundantly above all that we ask or think, according to the power that worketh in us," by faith.

There is power, dunamis power, of the Holy Spirit contained in the Life and DNA of God. We can **speak** (prophesy) that power into and onto another person (Acts 8:17). We can **pray** that power into and onto another person (II Tim. 1:6, Acts 19:6). We can **preach** that power into and onto another person (Acts 2:40-41). Jesus said himself, "the words that I speak are spirit and life". Today He is in us by His shed blood. The blood of His father, God's DNA. He now speaks through us. Our words become spirit and life to the hearer. His "virtue" now rests in and upon His body the Church. We are to let that virtue flow out from us to a lost and dying generation. To a hurting and bruised humanity.

Chapter 4

Family....Matters

Another recent incident that bolstered and reinforced these truths in my spirit occurred in early 1999. My wife Gloria and I had been caring for my elderly mother since the passing of my father in 1996. Mom was a spirit-filled believer who really loved God and the things of God. She had always been a great blessing to my family and me during my days in Bible College and my travels as an evangelist.

Mom had suffered several small strokes in the early nineties and she had become somewhat immobile and was also left with a little dementia. She was never in any pain and didn't suffer from any diseases other than the effects of the strokes. Internally she was physically fit and sound. She demonstrated this with a very healthy appetite.

For the first four years, my wife and I provided all of her care. We fed and dressed her and assisted her in bathing. We helped her take her vitamins and various other dietary supplements. After a while, she became incontinent and lost the ability to help feed herself or eat any regular foods. One can imagine the toll this exacted from my wife and I *me* because of around the clock care. Not to mention the strain that all of this was putting on our marriage and ministry. Finally we had become pretty weary and frazzled.

We decided that we needed a respite. Anxiously we made plans to take a much needed ten-day vacation to southern California. We made arrangements for mom to be placed in a local nursing facility until our return. (I might add that mom was very much against our trip and began to behave cantankerously. She would become very belligerent and sullen at times).….enter the Dragon.

The nursing home staff informed me that this kind of behavior was not unusual for elderly loved ones who were being left in facilities. (yes, but not MY mom.) The staff assured us that everything would be alright and to go ahead with our plans and enjoy ourselves....we deserved it!

In hindsight, I now realize that mom was allowing a small seed of contamination to enter into her spiritual DNA. The works of the flesh only need an inch and they will try to muscle their way all the way in. The kingdom of darkness always needs an invitation to get that first foot in the door (Eph. 4:26-27). Mom was determined that she was not going to let us just "abandon" her and go traipsing off in the sun somewhere to enjoy ourselves. We did leave and drove down to San Diego, hoping to find a little rest and relaxation.

Upon arriving in San Diego we called the nursing home to check on mom. They told us that everything was fine and not to worry. Their only problem was a heat wave that Portland was experiencing that had driven the temperature into the nineties. We stayed in San Diego a day or so and then Gloria and I both began to feel a little uneasiness in our spirits. We both felt a strong urge to return to Portland immediately. We packed and left that night.

About halfway home we stopped and called the nursing home again to let them know we were on our way home. They informed us that my mother had suddenly taken a turn for the worse and was in pretty bad shape. She had been refusing to eat or drink during our absence. She was running a fever and her temperature was over 102. Mom had become dehydrated and her blood sugar was 350 and climbing. We prayed in the car and continued on.

We arrived at the nursing home just in time to see them loading mom into an ambulance to take her into the emergency unit at the local hospital. She had slipped into what they called a diabetic coma. We stopped the paramedics and laid hands on her and prayed in Jesus' name. Invoking the power of the blood and resisting the lies of the enemy. (I must insert here the fact that my mother had no history of diabetes and never in her life had any sugar problems. The visiting nurse that had been coming every week to our home had never indicated to us any concern about her blood sugar. Mom's geriatric physician had never diagnosed any type of problem with her sugar. Whatever was attacking her bloodstream now was satanic in origin.)

Gloria and I prayed and believed God and they took her on to the hospital. After a few days she came out of the coma and began to show signs of improvement. The doctor told us that mom was now diabetic and she would need to take daily doses of insulin probably for the rest of her life.

They taught my wife and I how to take blood samples from mom's fingers four times a day and read it for the sugar content. We were also instructed on how to give her the insulin injections morning and evening. The next week we took mom home again and right away we began to speak God's protection over her. The visiting nurse would come twice a week and do evaluations and report to the doctor.

Gloria and I settled back into our elder-care routine and were thankful and joyful that mom was still with us. Now we had the added chore of the daily insulin injections. Also mom's only source of nutrition was now a special liquid diabetic drink that she had to consume eight times a day like clockwork.

After about six months of being intimidated by the enemy in this fashion, the tide was about to turn. One Sunday morning the spirit of the Lord began to shake me in my chair as I sat meditating on the Word of God. I could hear His still small voice speaking to my inner man. "Doesn't the life and power of God flow in you and through you? Doesn't the life and power of God flow in and through your wife? Don't you have authority as a believer? Didn't Jesus pay the price for your mother's healing as well as her salvation? Aren't you command in the word to lay hands on the sick and see them recover? What about the power of agreement? Isn't there healing in the stripes and blood of Jesus? Isn't the "Greater One" living in you and in your mother? Doesn't His blood flow to and through your mother?".......I decided right then and there it was time for a spiritual "blood transfusion".

I jumped up from the chair and grabbed my wife by the hand. I told her it was time to tell the devil where to go! I was tired of his trespassing on God's property. I asked her to agree with me. We went into my mother's sickroom and began to take authority over the ungodly situation. We commanded her pancreas and other internal organs to line up with the Word of God. We withstood the lies of the enemy with the truth of God. We spoke life (ZOE) to her cells and bloodstream and organs. We laid hands on her in the Name of Jesus and spoke cleansing to her bloodstream. Cleansing by the blood of Jesus! Healing by the stripes of Jesus! Wholeness by the light of Jesus! Vitality by the life of Jesus!

Immediately a change began to take place. We sensed a shifting in the spirit realm. She looked a little brighter. We knew by revelation knowledge that the adjustment had been made. The healing had come in Jesus' name.

This all took place on a Sunday morning. The visiting nurse was scheduled to come on Tuesday morning. We continued to give mom her injections as prescribed by her physician. (Over time we had learned to be wise as serpents and harmless as doves.) When God does something it's not a maybe but a yes and everybody is going to know it!

When the Health Nurse came on Tuesday morning we all sat around the living room for a while making small talk. Finally she went into mom's room to give her the usual checkup. Some time passed and then the nurse rushed into the living room. "How often have you been checking your mom's blood sugar?" she asked. "According to the schedule you left with us. Four times a day." I replied. "Where is her insulin?" asked the nurse. "In the fridge" I said quietly. She retrieved the vial of insulin and held it up to the sunlight shaking it vigorously and staring intently at it. "How much have you been giving her each time?" she asked with a scowl. "Six cc's" I answered. "Well don't give her anymore.

She doesn't need it." she muttered. "I'm going to schedule an appointment with the geriatric center for tomorrow for her." Stated the nurse. "Something's happening here."

To make a long story a little shorter, after the doctor's appointment they took my mother off the insulin injections. Her body was now producing its own insulin. The pancreas was working fine. To my knowledge she never had problem with sugar again! I believe the Life (DNA) of God had intermingled with her natural blood's life-flow once again and regulated things and brought things back into order and back into Divine Government. Glory! HIS Kingdom was once again in do-minion (the dominant gene). Even though she spent the last year of her life in a home for the aged, God had proven Himself faithful to His word in mom's life.

Mom graduated to be in the presence of the Lord in November of 2000 without the insulin injections. As a matter of fact, without any major disease. She caught a cold, quit eating and slept away. She was 89 years old. God indeed had satisfied her with long life (Psalms 91:16 – "with long life will I satisfy him, and show him my salvation").

With the knowledge of His DNA (blood) within us, mixed with faith:

Cancer cannot stay!

Diabetes cannot stay!

Blood dis-orders cannot stay!

All of these "dis-orders" must move back into order. His Divine order.

Chapter 5

A Heavenly Gene Pool

The DNA of God comes to us in the person of the Holy Spirit. That spirit is the Spirit of Truth (John 14:17). Truth, light and love all go together hand in hand. You can't have one without the other. Jesus Christ as He walked this earth declared that He was the Light (John 1:4). He also said that He was the Truth. Scripture also reveals that God is Love. Therefore His DNA comes to cause us to walk in the truth, to walk in the light and to walk in love. To truly be **led by the spirit** is to be led by love, light and truth, for the Spirit is all of these things. He (Holy Spirit) said that He would lead us and guide us into **all** truth (John 14:16-26). "As many as are led by the Spirit, they are the **Sons (and daughters)** of God." If you are really born into His family – the family of God – you will hear His voice and not hearken to the voice of another shepherd. If you have been truly born again (begotten from above) there is a substance within you that comes straight from the **throne room of the Father** and as you learn and grow and mature in your new nature (DNA), it will become virtually impossible for you to be deceived by the doctrines of devils (Matt. 24:24). "**If** it were possible" the very elect – those with the DNA of God – would be deceived. There will be a "connect" when you hear the real things of God, and a "dis-connect" in your spirit when you hear the things of the kingdom of darkness. What fellowship has the darkness with the light?

The Holy Spirit, (the carrier of God's DNA) has a real, tangible substance that comes upon us and into us. When this truth is imparted to our inner man **by the Spirit**, we move into another dimension of God. A new level of experience. A supernatural existence. He (the Holy Spirit) is real.

Just as real as the cloven tongues of fire on the day of Pentecost. Just as real as the sound of the mighty rushing wind. He comes to live with us and in us as a comforter and guide. As a carrier of God's DNA and genes. Ever present with us to lead and guide us into all truth. To empower us to be witnesses of Jesus Christ in all the earth.

Because of His genetic makeup in us we become more and more like Him. Doing the things in the earth realm that He would do. Because of this "dominant gene factor" we are renewed day by day in our inner man (the new man) (II Cor. 4:16). Because of this genetic code being implanted in us by His Spirit we are able to become **con-formed** to the image of Christ. Not conformed to this world's image but transformed (meta) by the renewing of our minds and hearts (Rom. 12:2).

That's why we act more and more like our Father as the days go by. We have been born of His incorruptible seed (I Pet. 1:4). When we become born again we draw from a new "gene pool". A "heavenly gene pool". Day by day His gene input becomes more and more the dominant gene factor in our lives. We begin to take on the Father's characteristics. The Father's personality. The Father's attributes.

(Divine Nature Attributes – DNA). The fruit of the Father's Spirit. We have been spiritually "genetically encoded" to possess **love**. We can't help but exhibit **joy**. We take on **peace**, moment by moment. **Longsuffering, gentleness and goodness** are our portion. We operate in a realm of **faith** with **meekness** and **temperance**. There is no law in the earth realm that can come against these spiritual fruit because they are the DNA (Divine Nature Attributes) of God (Gal. 5:22).

His incorruptible seed is in us, working to do His will and good pleasure (Eph. 1:5). For this cause we are conquerors and more than conquerors. We have a Divine connection to the planet called Heaven and we can draw upon its resources by faith whenever the need arises. Your new Spiritual Genetic Makeup demands that you overcome. Your new Spiritual Genetic Makeup demands that you walk in heavenly places.

Jesus was the "firstborn of many brethren" (Rom. 8:29). Since He's the elder brother, and He acts and talks just like the Father, and within Him were all the prophets, kings and priests, shouldn't we act and talk like our elder brother? We are partakers of His Divine nature. Let us lay down our earthly bloodline ties and take on our heavenly bloodline and nature. Let's take on our Father's mindset. "Let this mind be in you that was also in Christ Jesus...." (Phil. 2:5).

In the natural realm, or the earth realm, a child can't help but produce traces of his natural father and mother's gene pool. Hair color, eye color, skin tone, body type, etc. All things are parallel. This world is but a reflection of what happens in the spiritual (Rom. 1:20). So, in the spiritual realm, a true child of God can't help but produce the traits of his Father's gene pool.

When you are born into the family of god, you come in as a babe in Christ. You may not have a lot of defined family traits at this stage. However, in the natural realm a child grows day by day and matures. It takes on more and more of the characteristics of its father. Day by day it begins to look and act more and more like the father. So it is also in the spiritual kingdom. The spiritual child grows day by day....renewed day by day...being conformed to His image. The image of God.

If you are born again by the Spirit of God into the family of God, then you have inherited the **Kingdom Gene Pool**. You can't help but succeed! It's in your **genes**! You must come out a winner! It's in your **genes**! You will be an over comer. Why? Because it's in your **genes**! Your children shall flourish! Why? Because it's in your **genes** and you pass it on to them. You shall be the head and not the tail! It's in your **genes**. All people shall call you **blessed**! Because it's in your **genes**! You will love everybody because it's in your **genes**! If you have your Father's spiritual **genes** in you it will be easy for you to **pay your tithes and give freewill offerings**!

Begin to see things out of your Father's eyes. Take on His vision. I want people to be able to say, "he's got his father's eyes". I want them to say "he's looking more and more like his father". Let's look at others as God sees them. Let's say what God would say about a matter. Let's endeavor to think the thoughts that God would think about others. He would think **"good thoughts and not evil"** . 29:11). You have your Father's eyes. It's time to see the "big picture". Because of whose you are and who's in you, you have the unique ability to see things, situations and people as God sees them. You see **yourself** as God sees you! More than a conqueror....King and Priest....gloriously and wonderfully made...the head and not the tail!

Spiritual genetics is also a matter of the heart. "For with the heart man believeth unto righteousness" (Rom 10:9). There must be a **"love connection"** to make it a family affair. "Behold, what manner of **love** the Father has bestowed upon us, that we should be called the **sons** of God" (I John 3:1b). "Out of the **abundance of heart** the mouth speaketh" (Matt. 12:34). "For out of the **heart** flow the issues of life" (Prov. 4:23). Abundance means the dominant factor. The dominant gene. God's genetic order. "The mouth speaketh". To talk the love talk that the Father talks we need His love genes in us by the Holy Spirit. It's not hard to love our spiritual family members (brothers, sister, fathers and mothers) when we have been born into that family by love. His Divine Love. His DNA (Divine Nature Affection). His love or His nature within us, constrains us. Why? Because we are following after our spiritual genetic blueprint. The Father has **high** expectations for us. "For I know the thoughts that I think toward you, saith the Lord, thoughts of peace, and not evil, to give you an expected end." (Jer. 29:11).

Because of our Spiritual Genetic Makeup we have been **pre-destined** and **foreordained** before the foundations of the world to prosper and be in health even as our souls prosper.

This is a family affair. It's time we know whose genes are in us, recognize our DNA and stand tall. Taking our rightful place. Seated with Christ Jesus in heavenly places.

Chapter 6

Spiritual Genetics

Signs, wonders, miracles and healings are not the abnormal or SUPER natural for the Spirit filled believer but the natural or normal Christian life. For these are but the pattern of things that take place in our spiritual birthplace and homeland....a planet called Heaven. These are being worked out here in the earth realm.

According to scripture, when we are born again (Greek – "gennethe anothen" – begotten from above), (John 3:3) we become a new "species"; creation; being. We are truly not of this world. We came from Heaven…and we brought the Kingdom with us here to the earth realm. Now we are sojourners, passing through, shedding His Kingdom abroad as we occupy till He comes again to the earth and makes all things right.

Because we have been redeemed or brought back by the blood of Jesus, we must come to realize that our ability and our creativity are only limited by our faith in the atoning (cleansing DNA) process of that precious blood.

If fallen man in his unregenerated state (contaminated and tainted DNA) using only 10% of his brainpower can accomplish such feats as space travel and atomic nuclear energy…creating something out of almost nothing…how much more the **regenerated**, blood washed, blood bought sons and daughters of the creator of the universe have the capacity to perform once we realize our true **potential** and **purpose** and **power**.

In Genesis 1, the Spirit, or Life of God moved upon the face of the deep (chaos) and divided the waters from the waters. Dry land appeared and He caused light to come out of the darkness. He put the different strata of atmosphere into place and so on. Would not reasoning dictate that an entity with that kind of awesome power and authority and creative ability possess power enough to bring order and stability into your world and the world of those around you? You must **let** Him.

Acts the 28th chapter records an event concerning the Apostle Paul's experience with the DNA of God. The Apostle Paul was a born again, spirit-filled believer who knew who he was in God and also knew who God was in him. He was a man of faith and dedication to the cause of Christ. Following his born again experience on the road to Damascus, Paul went on to "bear much fruit and see that fruit remain".

On this particular occasion Paul and his fellow ship-mates had been shipwrecked on the Island of Melita. It was cold and rainy and as night fell they built a campfire and gathered around it to warm themselves. Men from the island joined them as everyone huddled close to the heat. As the Apostle leaned over to place some additional logs on the fire, a poisonous snake (pit viper) struck out and fastened itself to his hand. With the snake hanging onto his hand the Apostle Paul began to shake it off into the fire. For the next few minutes all eyes were on Paul because those men fully expected him to swell up and drop dead within a very short time. It is said that pit vipers' poison swells the human body up twice its size and brings death within three to four minutes. Those Eastern men knew that Paul would surely die. There was no snake anti-venom medicine available nor was their a snakebite kit among the shipwrecked items.

Everyone was waiting for Paul's blood to coagulate and thicken. They waited for the sweating and difficulty in breathing to begin. The Apostle's blood however had been infused with the DNA of God in the person of the Holy Ghost. His immune system and his poison defense mechanism were supernaturally (above natural or earthly laws and limitations) accelerated and destroyed the invading toxins in a matter of seconds. Get out of God's property...you are trespassing. Glory to God!

When we are born again we are born of the Spirit and the Blood. Immediately we begin to take on our NEW Father's nature. Divine DNA. When we are baptized with the Holy Ghost and Fire we receive an overwhelming impartation of the very Life and Nature of God. His DNA...Divine Nature Abilities...and we can know that we are His and He is mine!

Accordingly we need that "overwhelming impartation" of His DNA to become powerful witnesses of Jesus Christ. That's why we must wait upon the Holy Spirit until we are endued with "power from on high". Power from our spiritual birthplace or home. Christ commanded the early Church to wait upon the promise (Acts 1:8). We also must wait until we are spiritually "genetically engineered" by the Holy Ghost...fit for the battle! Ready to cast out devils, raise the dead, heal the sick, cleanse the leper, preach the Gospel to the poor, withstand poisons and toxins, and make disciples of all nations. It's only after this great infusion of His DNA that we come to know our authority over the natural and spiritual realm of this earth. That portion of God's spirit, DNA, that comes to every believer at the New Birth is immensely augmented when one is "endued with power from on high".

Spiritual Genetics provides you and I, the believer, with "Spiritual Clothing". Clothing from on high. We become clothed upon with Christ. We become clothed with Holy Fire. We are clothed with the Holy Ghost (Acts 2:1-4). We have a heavenly suit covering this clay suit. A suit of clothes better than any we could purchase at the finest apparel shop.

We are clothed in the Beauty of Holiness, more beautiful than the most fashionable garments of the day.

Our spiritual garments will keep out sickness and destruction. A spiritual suit of clothes. The three Hebrew boys in Daniel the third chapter wore such a suit. A suit that covers both inside and out. The Holy Ghost will come upon you and in you. When King Nebuchadnezzar heated the furnace seven times hotter than normal, he had no idea that the temperature of the furnace would have no bearing upon the DNA, or life, or Spirit of the Living God. The Spirit of God became a flameproof covering for Shadrach, Meshach and Abednego's natural bodies. God's DNA is eternal. God's DNA is indestructible. God's DNA is unquenchable. God's DNA is from everlasting to everlasting. His garments are better than asbestos. His armor is mightier than any metals or synthetics man can manufacture. He will keep you in the midst of your fiery trials if you will only trust in Him and apply His Life and substance to your situation by faith. His blood deems you an over comer. With God's Holy Spirit covering upon us and within us, miraculous things will occur.

Sampson wore such a "suit of the Spirit" into battle (Judges 4:6, 19, 15:8, 14). In the Old Testament the Holy

Ghost would come upon the saints of old by faith in the promise of the redemption purchased by the blood of Christ. When Sampson was clothed in this Holy armor he was invincible. The Spirit would move upon him and he would do mighty exploits. Now we can have this Spirit in an indwelling presence. A continuous access to the things of God and His Kingdom through His DNA (Divine Nature Access). His armament for us today consists of Spiritual things: a salvation helmet, a righteousness breastplate, Gospel of peace shoes, a truth girdle and a faith shield (Eph.6).

Philip's suit of the Spirit was able to teleport him from one place to another in the physical (Acts 8:39-40). After sharing the truth about Jesus with the Ethiopian eunuch, and baptizing him in the river, Philip was caught up **by the Spirit** and transported to his next revival in Caesarea. The spiritual genetic ability of the Father's Kingdom will and can help you also to see effective ministry in **your** life. Ministry that enjoys **maximum effectiveness with minimum weariness**. But you've got to move on into the supernatural, and then move on into the super supernatural!

God gave Adam a "clothing" of animal skins. He gives us a clothing of power of His Spirit and His Blood (DNA).

It was God's DNA that allowed the Old Testament saints to be transported by His spirit from one place to another. His DNA (Divine Nature Access) empowered them to be able to supercede the laws of science and nature. Over the course of my thirty years in ministry, I've seen and heard of many instances, here and on the mission field, of God miraculously intervening to save the lives of missionaries or bringing about Divine provision in the time of need. All of these things were done by His Spirit. That Life of God that He imparts to us at New Birth. We are the lights of this world but we must KNOW that in our hearts of hearts. We must know that His Light and His Life and His Love flow through us on a continual basis because we have His DNA in us.

God's protection and provision has saved my health and my life on more than one occasion. While on a missionary campaign in the country of Honduras, His divine providence was made real to me in a very dramatic way.

We were preaching and teaching throughout Honduras and ultimately wound up in Tecucigalpa, the capitol city. Multitudes of people were being saved, healed and delivered by the power of God. Miracles of every description were taking place as people forsook their idolatry and religious tradition and turned to a Living God.

A Pastor friend in Tecucigalpa, told us about an Island people called the Caribs who lived on the "Isles de Bahia". We felt led to go there to minister and the Spirit of Lord met us there. On our last day on the islands my co-evangelist and I had an encounter with the local witch doctor. He stood blocking our paths as we attempted to cross a rope bridge that stretched across a chasm that was literally an open sewer for the small seaside villages. This ditch carried the human waste from the stilt houses down to the sea.

When we were midway the bridge the ropes suddenly gave way and my friend and I plunged down into the filth below. Whether the bridge snapped as a result of the witch doctor's chanting, I'm not sure. It remains a mystery.

During our time on the Caribbean coast I had taken the opportunity to do quite a bit of snorkeling and my skin was badly cut from the razor sharp coral reefs. As we were pulled out I thought about the thousands of tiny little amoeba and bacteria that were attacking my open wounds. As we crawled the final few feet out of the ditch I whispered "clean in Jesus' Name" and the Spirit of God (DNA) spoke and said, "head for the sea". We both ran with all our might to the water and plunged in fully clothed.

Neither my co-evangelist nor myself suffered any ill effects of being in contact with all the germs and bacteria associated with that ditch. God's DNA and his divine protection insulated us from any dis-ease or infection the enemy had prepared for us. We arrived back in the United States praising God for the many victories wrought by His hand among the people of Honduras.

He will continue to perform "miracles" on the mission field and elsewhere because He is the God of the miraculous. Missionaries will continue to be saved from danger by some un-explicable twist of nature, or the bending of the laws of "science". God is the basis for all the sciences because everything that was made was made by Him for His good pleasure. Things seen and unseen. Things on the earth, in the earth, and over the earth (Col. 1:16). Alcoholics and substance abusers will continue to have encounters with his Spirit and the chemical makeup of their natural bodies will be altered. Why? Because his Spirit fashioned us and knows all about us. Every hair on our heads have been numbered by the Lord (Matt. 10:30). It is His will that all would be saved and none perish.

I once read the story of John G. Lake, the Apostle to Africa who lived in the early part of the twentieth century. One very amazing portion of the story was set in South Africa in 1910. A terrible plague was ravishing the country and about 1/3 of the population had been wiped out. Lake and his team members were helping out the local health teams by rounding up all the dead bodies they could find and burying them. All the while they were doing this none of them ever became sick with the plague or its symptoms. When questioned about what he was doing to keep the plague from affecting him Lake replied, "Brother, it is the law of the Spirit of Life in Christ Jesus. I believe that just as long as I keep my soul in contact with the living God so that His Spirit is flowing into my soul and body, that no germ will ever attach itself to me, for the spirit of God will kill it."

After telling them this, John G. Lake then invited them to test out what he said by conducting an experiment. He had them gather mucous from the lungs of the dead and examine it under a microscope. They did and found millions of germs alive and swarming in each batch. He then had them smear the mucous over his hands and declared to them that all of the germs would fall dead because of the power of Holy Spirit.

As they continued to watch under the microscope, the germs fell dead instantly and everyone in the room was astonished at the miracle. John G. Lake knew beyond a shadow of doubt that the very DNA (Divine Nature Ability) of God rested within. He knew that it was this same Spirit of the Living God that was transmitted to the sick bodies of those that he prayed for and commanded healing in the Name of Jesus. It is said that while he resided in the city of Spokane, Washington that it was the healthiest city in America because John G. Lake wasn't afraid to impart the DNA of God, the healing and saving ability of the Most High God to all those who were in need. Jesus said, "Greater works than these will you do because I go unto my Father." (John 14:12).

The Bible tells us that our bodies are the "temples of God". The Holy Spirit lives in our temples and Christ lives in our temples and God the Father lives in our temples by His DNA (I Cor. 5:19, Rom. 8:11, II Cor. 6:16, Eph. 3:17,

Col. 1:27). You and I contain the very ZOE life of God, that eternal DNA of the Father, the indwelling Life of Creation in our bodies and spirits. Having God's DNA in us brings the **favor** of God into our lives. **Favor** is better than money. You can spend all of your money, but you can never spend all of God's **favor**. Therefore let us use that **favor** to bless others. Let us **impart, impact and improve** the lives of those we come in contact with on a daily basis.

We have a God given (inherited) ability to invent and create machinery and devices and witty inventions (Prov. 8:12, II Pet. 1:3). We have a God given (bloodline) ability to create something from nothing (Heb. 11:1). We have a God given ability to succeed in business and all things pertaining to life and Godliness (II Pet. 1:3).

Chapter 7

It's in Your Genes

Whan the revelation of the Life of God (ZOE) –
His ability and His accessibility – becomes truth
in your spirit man, it's time for you to implement what I like
to call the RAM principle. RAM is an acronym for
Revelation, Activation and Manifestation.

If we speak to our bodies and our circumstances using
that Divine authority (DNA) given to every believer by the
Father…we too can walk in Divine Health, enjoy prosperity
and overcome the enemies of God. We must become

convinced of the integrity of God's word. If He said it then it's **true**. Let God be true and every man a liar. Never mind those who will tell you that healing and miracles are not for today. The bible says Jesus Christ the same yesterday, today and forever (Heb. 13:8). He still hates sin. He still hates sickness and dis-ease. He still hates lack and poverty. And if He's in us we will hate those things also and will do every-thing we can to eradicate them from the face of this planet. Jesus taught us to pray that the Kingdom of God or the Kingdom of Heaven would come to this earth. That God's will would be done in the earth as it is being done in the heavenlies. This can and will be brought about. And you can be a part of making it a reality (Matt. 6:9-13).

There is an awe inspiring revival taking place in Africa, South America and other so-called third world nations of the world at the time of this writing. Literally millions of people are turning to the Lord and giving themselves over to God. The Father is birthing spiritual things into the lives of countless numbers of people all because they dare to believe Him and take Him at His Word. They are seeing their dead being brought back to life...the blind receive their sight and the lame walk. People groups who had once been written off by the mainstream churches of the western world are raising up churches with memberships in the thousands and hundreds of thousands.

God is truly pouring out of His Spirit upon **all** flesh. He is pouring out of His DNA upon anyone willing to get under the spout. Most of these new "converts" don't have the resources or the time to stop and go to Bible College or enroll in "Successful Christian Living" classes, but I have noticed that it doesn't take them long to grasp a hold to the RAM principle. Once they hear the Word of God (**Revelation**) and it gets in their spirit man they move out on the Word (**Activation**) and they are seeing tremendous results (**Manifestation**). God's DNA in you will always respond to His Truths. Truth responding to Truth. The Holy Ghost will only testify of Him (John 15:26).

Because of whose you are and who's in you...you can ask what you will and it shall be done. Many years ago before I totally understood the complete workings of the DNA of God working in my life, God made it plain to me that His word is the final authority and nothing else really matters. You see His Word contains the very same DNA (Divine Nature Ability, Divine Nature Access, Divine

Nature Attributes) that His Spirit holds. His Word was with Him from the very beginning. His Word is Jesus, the Spirit of Prophecy.

My evangelistic team and I were in the midst of taking down a small gospel tent I owned after a wonderful tent crusade in the city of Geneva, New York. As I lifted my end of the big Hammond B3 organ I felt a sharp pain tear through my back and I dropped the organ and sat down to catch my breath. The others finished tearing down and loading up the equipment and I got into my car and drove the thirty miles or so to where we lived in Syracuse, New York.

Upon arriving home and cleaning up an awful weakness came over me and my wife suggested that I go and lie down. Well I did, and that's where I remained for the next two weeks. My temperature rose to over 102 and during the course of those first few days my weight dropped by about thirty or forty pounds to 100 lbs. I had no appetite and could barely even get water down. My strength was dissipated and all I did was lie there and wonder why me. We had just closed out a glorious campaign where people were saved and healed by the power of God.

This all took place in 1977 and I was a young evangelist who had never been sick or incapacitated. This was something new for me. A trial by fire. Little did I know that God was going to use this attack of the enemy to give me a little "experiential knowledge" of His healing grace.

My son Tim Jr. was only about 5 or 6 at the time and he would come and stand at my bedside and ask me if there was anything he could do for me or was there anything I wanted. I could only shake my head and close my eyes again and lick my parched lips. I knew that he didn't understand what was wrong with daddy because I didn't either. I only knew that I preached healing and deliverance and God would have to heal me as he had done for so many others in our meetings.

Satan can be very vicious in his attacks against the people of God but no weapon formed against us shall prosper as long as we maintain a **DNA match**. He is a defeated foe and the keys have been taken from him and given to the Church. Things really were not good at this time and my body was taking a beating. Every time I went to the restroom blood would pass from my body like a fountain.

I knew that the Bible said that the blood contained the life. I could see my life being flushed down the toilet. Satan whispered, "You are dying. You will never preach again. I've got you now". My temperature continued to rise and I had no appetite whatsoever. It felt as though the lower half of my body was on fire. All was not lost however because God almighty was still in control and as long as he is in control, it's got to turn out all right.

I was soon to experience the impartation of God's DNA (Divine Nature Ability) through the laying on of hands. Something I had administered many times, however I had not been on the receiving end of very often.

After more than ten days of this my wife let me know in no uncertain terms that she was beginning to be really concerned and suggested that I go to the hospital at least so we'd know what we praying about. I finally capitulated and agreed.

Due to my lack of strength I had to be carried to the car by our neighbor Mitch. He picked me up in His arms and took me and laid me in his station wagon. I certainly didn't feel like God's man of faith and power at that moment. But the DNA of God the Farther was still alive in me and it was feeding my spirit man with faith and patience. Mitch drove us to Crouse/Hinds Memorial Hospital and put me in a wheelchair and took me into the emergency room.

After what seemed like many hours they finally came out and asked some questions and then took me in to be examined. The doctor took x-rays and ran blood tests and did everything else that doctors do to diagnose your condition. Several hours went by and then they came and took me back into the hallway in my wheelchair and left me to wait.

Late that evening a very pleasant young doctor came over to my wheelchair and kneeled beside me to give me the prognosis. He related to me that my prostate gland was swollen to the size of a baseball and it was infected and it looked like it was malignant. They wanted to do surgery as soon as possible. This was on a Sunday and they were going to let me go home and come back on Monday morning for the surgery. I was instructed not to eat anything and given some very large blue pills to take that were to help clean my system for the surgery (or something).

As you can imagine I wasn't a very happy camper on the way home. All sorts of thoughts were going through my mind. When we reached the house they carried me in and laid me on the bed again. My wife took my clothes off and covered me up with a blanket. I was feeling pretty miserable and sick and weak. The enemy was quietly reminding me that I had two uncles who had died with prostate cancer. He would suggest to me that it had something to do with my life before I met Jesus. What a **liar** he is. My spirit inside kept rebutting the enemy with verses of scripture. The devil cited the statistics concerning the prostate cancer rate among African-American men in the United States. He was trying to call my bluff with information. The only information I could truly rely on was the revelatory Word of God (His DNA) ZOE!

About that time my son entered the room to see how I was doing. The sight of him caused the **joy** of the Lord to leap up within my bosom. "I'll be alright" I assured him. I asked him to hand me my Dakes Bible from the night stand. When he plopped that big, black Bible up onto my chest it fell open to the book of James the 5th chapter. I began reading the 13th through the 15th verses. "Is any among you afflicted? Let him pray. Is any merry? Let him sing songs. Is any sick among you? Let him call for the elders of the

Church; and let them pray over him, anointing him with oil in the name of the Lord. And the prayer of faith shall save the sick, and the Lord shall raise him up; and if he hath committed sins they shall be forgiven him."

Wow. It was as if the very DNA of God leaped from those pages into my spirit man. The truth of God's Word connected with His truth in me (Holy Spirit). The life and light and love of the Father were rekindled within and I felt faith arise in my soul. We possess a heavenly treasure within these earthen vessels. Something sent from heaven above. Not of this world, but of another realm. My heart began to race with excitement. Strength began to come back into my body. (I believe that the healing was initiated even then as I read the Word of the Living God). This was the first step in the RAM principle. **Revelation.**

I shouted for my wife to come in the room and instructed her to get on the phone and call my Dad and my uncle. My dad was a deacon with a gift ministry that had planted three churches in the upstate New York area. My uncle Dee Smith was a pastor who also was blessed with a gift ministry. He was also the District Superintendent for their denomination. They both lived in Rochester,

New York, which was about ninety miles from Syracuse. It would take them a while to get there and it was Sunday night and they both had just left church services. **Activation**.

Late that night they arrived and rushed to my room to see what the problem was. I explained to them what the doctors had told me and rehearsed what I had read in James. Without hesitation they had the oil out and were quizzing me as to whether there was any thing I needed to confess or let go of. "Not that I know of" was my reply. Before I knew it, oil was being poured on my head and hands were being laid on the top of my head and the base of my spine.

Instantly I felt the DNA of God...that Life giving substance from Heaven...that light that comes into your inward parts by the Holy Ghost...the very breath of Christ overshadowed my entire being. It seems as though His blood drenched me from head to toe and I knew He was there with me. Their prayer was direct and to the point and very loud and animated. In minutes they were done and looked me in the eye and said, "it's done."

Dad and Uncle Dee didn't waste a lot of time trying to shore up my faith or encouraging me to hold on.

They believed it had been accomplished by faith. The God kind of faith. The ZOE kind of faith. The kind of faith that comes with the DNA (Divine Nature) of God. They knew from experience that they possessed the genetic ability of God in them. They knew from experience that it was in their genes and they could pass it on to others in various ways. They knew that the spirit within them was a power that passes all understanding and reasoning. **Manifestation**.

As soon as they had walked out the door to begin the long drive home my son, Tim Jr., came back into the room with wide-eyed curiosity. "Son," I breathed, "go in the kitchen and tell your mother to fix my supper. Tell her I want a big plate because I'm really hungry. Some collard greens and yams, and some smoked meat and potato salad. Oh yeah, and a sixteen ounce Pepsi so cold that there's a frost on the bottle." He scampered out to the kitchen and I sat up in bed and smiled one of those 'I'm so glad I know Jesus smiles'. I was instantly healed by the power of God. My appetite was back and my strength returned. The hemorrhaging ceased and I was back preaching that next week. It was in my genes to be healed. It was in Dad's genes to impart healing. It was in Uncle Dee's genes to believe for healing. What a mighty God we serve!

That was decades ago. I never returned to the doctor and I haven't been bothered with prostate trouble again. Some may say, well it's still there, it's just in remission. Well I've got news for them. IF it is still there...which it is not...but IF it was still there it wouldn't be in REmission it would be in SUBmission. Submission to the Dominant gene factor in my life, the blood and authority of Jesus. By whose stripes I was healed a long time ago. You have within you the very essence of all that God is and all that He wants you to be. No corrupt thing shall enter therein!

This is a new day. Filled with the Revelation Knowledge of Kingdom Technology and Kingdom Principles. We have taken on a new concept of who God is and how he deals with His people. We know more about who we are in Him than our forefathers because He is revealing His attributes and character to us in new ways. He is restoring our contact with Divine Government and Theocratic living in this hour. Blessed be the Name of the Lord. These are exciting times to be ALIVE in Him. His Holy Spirit is ushering in His Second coming to this earth realm.

These days I rise up early in the morning with His praises on my lips. After a few hours of worship and devotions and prayer, I minister to myself. I maintain my walk in Divine Health by speaking words of Spirit and Life over my body and the bodies of my wife, children and grand children. I speak with authority to my bloodstream and my organs on a daily basis. I call this taking my vitamins. I remind my cells and my organs that because of Christ's complete work on the cross they now have to remain subject to the Divine laws of God. My temple is completely governed by His authority. The blood and stripes of Jesus bound this in heaven and loosed light and health upon the earth. Amen.

Chapter 8

Divine Connection

The supernatural Divine Nature Ability (DNA) of the Holy spirit is available to anyone who will ask for it. Jesus said seek and you will find...ask and it shall be given...knock and the door shall be opened unto you. God's desire is to have sons and daughters here on the earth to love Him and worship Him in Spirit and in Truth

He wants us to enjoy the benefits of Divine health and divine providence. It's His will that we partake of His Divine Protection and Provision. The same miracle working power of God that was exemplified in the Old Testament scriptures is available to us here and now. He wants us to prosper and be in good health (III John 2).

Throughout the Old Testament we can read stories of how God supernaturally showed Himself strong on behalf of His people. Believe it or not, He's dong the same thing today. The Hebrew children were sent into slavery in Egypt but they had a blood contract or covenant with Jehovah God. They were under the covering of His DNA (Divine Nature Ability, Divine nature Access, Divine Nature Attributes) even under the taskmasters of the Egyptian Pharaoh. By faith in the PROMISE of a redeemer, they were able to tap into the genetic pool of God and become his sons and daughters. They obtained access to Kingdom technology that the Egyptians in all of their wisdom could not comprehend.

By shedding the blood of goats and bullocks and looking forward in time to the Blood of the Lamb of God, they were included into the inheritance of the saints. Even under the stress and duress of bondage and slavery in Egypt, God's people...that were called by His name...flourished and were fruitful and multiplied. They waxed strong and grew in number and wisdom an strength. God's Holy Spirit was there in the desert with them. He never left them or forsook them. His light and love and life was nestled in among the brick making ovens and the Egyptian masters. In the face of that kind of adversity God's people... His family...His Genos (connected genetically)...not only survived but went on to become great and mighty. They went into bondage fifty strong and came away almost a million strong.

You, dear reader, can also come out of your adverse situation bigger than when you went in if you will keep covenant with God of this universe. If you will acknowledge Him in all of your ways and seek His face and keep his laws...don't mingle with the gods of this world, but keep yourself connected to the vine...then you can stand still and see the Salvation of the Lord. By faith in the Blood of Jesus you can inherit the DNA of God. The power of DO-minion and overcoming in this earth realm.

God's Divine provision and protection are part and parcel of family membership. And it does not matter who you are or where you come from. God has no respect of person (Acts 10:34). The DNA of God is universal.

God's DNA can be found in every tribe, kindred, tongue and nation on the face of the earth. Once a person is "born again" or "begotten from on high", they are translated out of their natural ethnic bloodline and "adopted" or "grafted into" the Spiritual bloodline of Father God. The family of God goes **beyond culture**. It supercedes ethnicity. White people's blood can become infused with the DNA of God. Black people's blood can become infused with the DNA of God. Yellow people's blood can become infused with the DNA of God. From the North Pole to the South Pole and from the Orient to the Western world, God's DNA can be detected in all of those who have chosen to believe on Jesus Christ and the Power of His blood. More amazing, all of his children worldwide know and love one another because of "like DNA".

The answer to the so-called "race" problem in the world today is the revelation of the DNA of God. There is but one global "race". The race of mankind or the "human race". This race began when God breathed the "breath of lives" into Adam at creation. All of the differences that we see and talk about (skin color, language, body characteristics, etc.) are tribal, ethnic or cultural differences within the one human race. These differences came into being after the great dispersion at Babel (confusion) when mankind was scattered over the face of the earth. Currently there are only two types or classes in the world...**regenerated and unregenerated**!

Once a person is "born again", or in other words regains the DNA of Father God, he reassumes the innate knowledge of God's creation and once again becomes color blind and culture blind. That's how the early Church at Antioch could be made up of various ethnic groups (Acts 1). Even the leadership was made up of various ethnic groups. After the early Jewish brethren were made aware by God Himself that ethnicity would not play a part in ones receiving the DNA of God, the Church became a literal melting pot. Jews, Greeks, Africans, Romans, Samaritans, Cretians and on and on and on. They all had one thing in common. The DNA (ZOE life) of God that put them into the same "genos" or family. They were first called Christians – imitators of Christ – at Antioch.

Instead of looking to the world or the world's system and institutions to deal with the so called "race" issue, maybe some of the solution can come from the true Church of Jesus Christ. The body of Jesus. "Judgment begins at the House of God." When **we**, the family of the Most High God, begin to reflect the ethnic diversity of our cities and towns in which we erect our Houses of Worship…when **we** begin to tear down the walls of prejudice and bigotry within our ranks and within our **leadership**…when Sunday morning is no longer the most segregated hour of the week in our nation…then and only then can we expect to see change in the unregenerated or so called sinner whose nature is to pre-judge and hate because he has the nature of his father the devil.

We are the children of the light and the children of his love. Begotten **in** His Love and **by** His love. We possess a new and different nature. A nature of love and harmony. A nature that **compels** us to see people more as **"worth"** than as **"who"**. A nature or family identity that **compels** us to especially love the brethren. The household of faith. Any brethren and **all** the brethren. Then the world will know that we are his children by our love one to another.

If we will maintain that intimacy with the Beloved and cancel out any hindrances to our maintaining a good DNA "match", He said ask what you will and it shall be done.

The DNA of God will multiply those things we have and cause supernatural provision in the time of need. We may be heading for some rough times in the near future, but God has promised to take care of his own (Heb. 13:5b). We must walk in love and honesty and purity of heart. The rewards for so doing will be too numerous and wonderful to describe.

I'm reminded of a God-incidence that happened years ago in the early years of our ministry that let me know our God is the God of enough. El Shaddai. Jehova Rohi. The Lord is our Shepherd and His life and DNA will work miracles in our midst. We had been doing a lot of ministry among the Puerto Rican community in upstate New York and we had become close friends with many of them. As a matter of fact, a Latin Gospel Band by the name of Noah's Ark had traveled with us to some of our evangelistic crusades. Also, I would frequently be the guest speaker at the annual Puerto Rican Festival and the band members would join me in ministry at the altar call. We were really good friends and they would be over to our house quite a bit rehearsing or just hanging out.

On this particular occasion, some of the fellows and their families had come over after the morning worship service and we were praising God and enjoying the fellowship of one another. It started with about five of us. Every fifteen or twenty minutes the doorbell would ring and we would be joined by another family and friends. This went on for a while until there were thirty-five or forty people in the place. Some were inside and some were outside. Some were upstairs and some were downstairs.

My wife had already cooked dinner and it was on the stove. A four-quart pot of spaghetti, a loaf of bread and a large pitcher of punch. Naturally we invited each family to help themselves as they entered the house. I figured all of the food would be gone after about the second family. Suddenly, (I really love the "suddenlies" of God) my wife came running down into the basement and whispered in my ear, "Come upstairs, you've got to see this!" She grabbed me by the arm and we rushed back upstairs. She reached over and took the lid off the spaghetti pot and lo and behold it was STILL FULL! "It stays just like this," she exclaimed. "The more everyone comes back and helps themselves the more it seems to fill right back up again!" We watched in reverent awe as my brothers and sisters enjoyed their meal and the sweet communion of the Holy Ghost.

When it was time for everyone to leave and I bid the last visitor farewell, I returned to the kitchen in time to see my wife standing there at the stove with tears in her eyes holding the lid to the pot in her hands whispering "There's still some left, there's still some left!"

Jesus Christ the same yesterday, today and forever! His Spirit had done for us just what He had done for the five thousand hungry souls some two thousand years ago (Luke 9:14). When you couple right living with faith and mix it with His Word and DNA (Spirit), you too can see the natural boundaries of science, logic and reason shattered by the almighty power of God!

I realize that the cessationists declare that physical miracles such as this do not happen today and were done way with after the establishment of the early Church…along with healing, miracles, tongues, prophecy, Apostles and Prophets…however, I would rather rely upon my own experiential knowledge then the theoretical suppositions of someone else.

Chapter 9

Contamination and Maintaining a Match

When Adam and Eve were in the Garden in an innocent and perfect state, it was spiritual adultery or spiritual fornication that tainted the perfect Holy DNA of God that was contained within their bloodstreams. They rebelled against the known or revealed will of God and listened to the voice of an outsider (Gen. 2). They committed treason against the Kingdom of God and the Kingdom of Light and received as recompense the entrance of the kingdom of darkness into their existence.

Death and destruction became what they had to look forward to. Go had placed them in an environment most conducive to their growth and fulfillment, a literal paradise. They chose to break out of the boundaries of this paradise by going against the will of the Maker and Creator of the Garden.

Tainted or contaminated DNA comes through "mixed blood". The origin for mixed blood coming into the picture is always spiritual adultery or spiritual fornication. Also the efficacy of the Divine substance is sometimes diminished because of **fear, doubt and unbelief**.

I can remember once when I needed a miracle from God and I had to fight to keep the pollution of fear and doubt from coming in and contaminating my spiritual DNA. God's Divine Nature Ability. My oldest son, Tim Jr. was in about the fifth grade and was attending a grammar school in Seminole County Florida. One day they called me in to the school and told me that Tim had hurt himself and needed to go to the hospital. When I arrived at the facility, Tim was in the nurse's office lying down. He had a hernia and it was really pretty ugly. His testicles had been pushed up out of the scrotum and were in the lower part of his abdominal cavity. He was in a lot of pain. The nurse informed me that he would need surgery or he could suffer dire consequences. They even mentioned the possibility of losing the ability to have children. My son was very dear to me and it pained me to see him in this condition but I knew that we needed to trust God in this situation.

After consulting the nurse and doctor over the phone I decided to take Tim home and pray for him to be healed. You would have thought that I set off the burglar alarm or something. Everyone became very hostile and began threatening me with legal action and so forth if I did not allow them to call an ambulance and take Tim to the hospital for surgery. While every one was scampering around and cursing me and calling me foolish I could hear the voice of the Lord saying **I am the GREAT physician.**

After some time the doctor came in and tried reasoning with me and tried to convince me that it would be in Tim's best interest to have the surgery. He talked about how he would not be able to participate in any sports if I did not take care of this now. He mentioned again the fact that his ability to have children would be just about zero if I didn't send him through the surgery. I knew that this was testing my belief system to the maximum.

Sometimes you have to really fight the good fight of faith to keep your spiritual DNA intact and free from the contaminations of **fear, doubt and unbelief**. It's especially difficult when it's not you but one of your loved ones who will have to live with the outcome of you decision. It has even more of an impact when it's your child.

Finally, the doctor said he respected me for my faith even though he disagreed with me and they decided to let us go. However, they had me sign a release form releasing them from any future liability should something tragic happen.

No sooner than we arrived home my wife met me at the door with the anointing oil and we anointed Tim and laid hands on him and prayed the prayer of faith. The power of the Holy Ghost saturated the room and the DNA of God came and touched my son. By His stripes he was healed. The Blood of Jesus had come to our rescue once again. There is power in the Blood of Jesus. There is power in the Name of Jesus. There is the DNA of God in the Word of God.

We lingered in the room for a while basking in the presence of the Lord. His essence was still there. There was a sweet smelling aroma of the Holy Spirit there with us. We worshiped and praised Him and sang songs and hymns until suppertime. Jesus the Healer lives in every true child of God today. Simply call upon His wonder working Divine Nature and you will experience restoration, renewal and revival.

My son was healed without having to go into surgery and all the Glory belongs to God. Two weeks after we prayed for him he came home from a youth activity group with a trophy almost as tall as he was. He had won first place in a "Break Dancing" contest. This was the boy they said would not be able to participate in athletics without an operation. Well he had an operation, an operation of the Holy Spirit. He went on to be one of the top young gymnastic contenders around. God's DNA can be imparted by the **laying on of hands**. Not only did he go on to have a normal childhood with God's favor and hand upon his life, but he also grew into a blessed adult with five beautiful children and a wonderful wife. (The medial profession had advised us earlier about the possibility of him becoming sterile without surgery). He is currently the Praise and Worship leader at a rapidly growing church in the Pacific Northwest, born again, Spirit filled and immersed in the DNA (Divine Nature Ability) of God.

If you will read through the books of First and Second Kings you will see that if you belong to the family of God…if you are counted among his people…the only one that can curse you or reverse the blessings of God upon your life is **you yourself** (Num. 23:8). The prophet could not curse whom God had blessed. If you are filled with the DNA of God you are blessed. There is nothing anybody can do about it no matter who they are. No matter how powerful or influential they may be they cannot reverse the blessing of God the Father.

The prophet could not curse what God had blessed, but the people could cause the curse to come upon themselves by contaminating the DNA of God. They could taint His genetic order by worshipping idols and pollute His gene pool by marrying strange wives who worshipped other gods. Spiritual adultery or fornication always contaminates the DNA of God. We need to remain in the place of safety by worshipping the only True God in Spirit and in Truth.

We also need to take a look at ourselves and make sure that our DNA is a "match" with the Fathers. Miracles, signs and wonders are contained within His gene pool. Praise and worship ought to be our daily diet if our DNA is a match. They should be our breast milk; our life source along with the word of God. The Holy Ghost is the seed of our life in God and we need to pass it on from generation to generation.

Peter and John were at the Gate Beautiful in Acts the third chapter when a crippled beggar asked them for some change. Their reply was silver and gold we don't have…however, we do have something valuable, the DNA of God. The Divine Nature of the Holy Ghost. The Divine Ability of God. The Divine Access to the things of His kingdom. We can draw upon that which we do have…rise up and walk! They lifted the man to his feet and he went away leaping and praising God never to beg again. The life source of God was in their **words**. The same creative power is in **your** words if you believe and recognize who you are and whose you are!

Within our Father's DNA is every thing we need pertaining to life and Godliness. As long as we continue to draw form His gene pool we are **conquerors**, we walk in **Divine Health**, we are **rulers over kingdoms and nations**, we are **divinely prosperous**, we possess **supernatural creative abilities** and we **master situations and circumstances**.

Because of your Spiritual Genetic Makeup, the environment most conducive to your productivity is a heavenly environment. A Kingdom environment. A Glory realm environment. An environment in His presence and in His glory. Stay there! Live there! God placed everything that He made in an environment most conducive to its growth and well being. Most conducive to its reproduction. He put fish in water. He put birds in the air and in trees. He put penguins in the snow. What about you and I? Let's stay where God puts us…in Him.

Stay in His presence. Stay before His face. You can build up your spiritual blood pressure and move from ENEMIC to DYNAMIC in a short while. Pray in the Holy Ghost. When you pray and worship in the spirit, speaking in heavenly languages and abandoning earthly boundaries, you not only build up your spirit man and yourself in your most holy faith, but you force your spirit man

(God's genes...His DNA) to become and remain dominant. Sickness and dis-ease (outlaw cells, viruses and bacteria) that have been trying to invade your earthly tabernacle (body) must be obedient to the law and authority of God and leave His dominion. Glory!

God has given each of us our own unique personal spiritual DNA that is unlike any other being ever created. Your individual, divine purpose or blue print is encoded in that DNA and it's unique to you...just like your fingerprint or your voiceprint. There is not an identical one like it in existence. He has encoded your spiritual DNA to respond individually to His love and His presence. That's why when you begin to praise and worship Him, even in the midst of millions of others praising and worshipping Him around the world, He hears **your** voice! Likewise, when you won't worship Him and give Him praise...He knows that also. When you won't praise Him and worship Him your voice is missing from that great crescendoing concert of worship that comes up before Him continually from the earth. He knows when a voice is missing from the choir of worship that ascends to Him daily as a sweet smelling savor of offering.

Isn't it amazing that scientist after years of studying and analyzing thousands of voice patterns and recordings have determined that no two voiceprints are identical? Your voiceprint is just like your fingerprint...exclusively yours. You can even be convicted in a court of law based upon voiceprint evidence. How awesome is our God! He hears us when we call...individually.

Your spiritual birthing environment has a lot to do with how your DNA is processed over time. Being birthed into an environment not conducive to growth and development will stunt the growth process. The end result being an underdeveloped and mal-formed adult sized believer. Still needing milk to nurture and strengthen the skeletal structure even though appearing to be fully matured.

Our bodies are the temples of the Holy Spirit. As long as we give Him free reign we are under Divine protection. His genes remain dominant. However, if we grieve Him (Holy Spirit) or quench Him with **fear, doubt and unbelief,** there is a possibility that we can encounter things in this life that have their origin in the kingdom of darkness.

Let us maintain a positive DNA "match" and partake of the fruit of His DNA residing within us...**love, joy, peace, longsuffering, gentleness, goodness, faith, meekness, temperance.** No other law (law of sin and death) can prevail against the fruit of the Spirit. It's a process (Gal 65:22). After receiving His DNA you WILL begin to manifest His fruit

DNA =

Divine Nature Access

Divine Nature Ability

Divine Nature Attributes

Divine Nature Activation

Divine Nature Affection...(Gal. 4:6, Gal. 3:21, Jude 20-22)

Steps to a Strong DNA:

1. Build up yourself in the most holy faith.

2. Pray in the Holy Ghost.

3. Continue to walk in love.

4. Walk in mercy and compassion.

Steps to maintaining a positive DNA match:

1. Fasting

2. Prayer

3. Study

4. Giving

5. Worship

Chapter 10

Blood Covenant

In this chapter we want to take a look at the Blood Covenant or Blood agreement that is such and integral part of the plan of salvation. We may look at it from a different perspective than we have in the past, simply because of the times in which we live. The fabric of the family is disintegrating right before our eyes and the sanctity of marriage has been all but lost in certain segments of our society from the least to the greatest among us.

One in two marriages end in divorce and single parent homes are almost the norm. Television and movies have offered alternatives to marriage with most of the couples featured in the most popular sit-coms these days simply choosing to live together.

What is most disturbing is that the Body of Christ appears to be sliding down that same slippery slope in this particular area of spiritual conflict. There is a need for the revitalization of the truths of God concerning covenants and contracts form a biblical perspective. There is no demand put upon unregenerate mankind to activate revelation knowledge in the earth today. But there is a demand put upon us, the people of God. Those of us who have the DNA of God working in us need to seek the Face of God until He answers and provides remedies of wisdom for the pain and suffering that this generation of earthly inhabitants have inflicted upon themselves.

There is so much rich, relevant and revealing information contained in the "mystery" of the Blood Covenant. From Genesis to Revelation there is this scarlet thread that runs the length, breadth, width and height of the Holy Word. I'm convinced that we've only known in part (I Cor. 13:9), the revelation of the Covenant between the Creator and His Creation – sealed in blood. The closer we get to the culmination of **this** age I see an expansion of spiritual revelation knowledge taking place. A greater degree of understanding of some of the types and shadows of scripture.

For instance, let's consider the institution of marriage between a man and a woman. I believe that it is to be a beautiful illustration of something spiritual and holy in the Kingdom of God. A token and a type in the earth realm of the Eternal Blood Covenant (Eph. 5:22-23).

We're living in an age when marriage, childbearing, life-time commitment and covenants have been so trivialized, that most of Western civilization (including a large number of spirit filled believers) never realizes the awesomeness and sanctity of these aspects here on the earth. There is some-thing deeply spiritual about the union of a man...created in the image of God...and a woman. The twain (two) becoming **one** flesh. When we grasp it in revelation truth, it takes on a much more sacred and holy connotation.

Let's begin by remembering the great and awesome privilege that Father God has bestowed upon all mankind. He has given us the opportunity to partner with Him in one of the most glorious and stupendous undertakings that has ever been conceived. **Creating life**. Replenish this great planet called Earth, with all of the universe and the countless galaxies as a witness. Working with Him to build and rebuild His handiwork! However spectacular and humbling that fact may be...that is not the end of it.

Everything that is "alive" or "living" on this planet has the capability to reproduce itself. If it's alive, it reproduces. If it does not reproduce, chances are there is no life in it. No DNA, the code of life. But unlike the various other life forms found on the Earth, man is the only life form **created in the image and likeness of Father God**. Think about that. God the Father has put within us, His creation, the ability to bring forth other life in His image and likeness. Oh how He must trust His creation. What a weighty privilege and responsibility He has entrusted to you and I. What manner of love is this? But that's not all.

Because every human being is created in God's image and likeness, unlike the plants and the animals, the **fruit** of our loins and the **fruit** of our wombs becomes **eternal fruit**. That's right, **ETERNAL**. What we bring forth into the earth realm has a soul. A soul that will live as long as God lives and He is eternal. A soul that will live forever. Throughout eternity. Either in the presence of Almighty God or separated from Him (eternal damnation which is the second death, Re. 21:8). What a sobering thought. "All souls are mine saith the Lord", (Eze. 18:4). God allows us to partner with Him in the business of bringing forth souls into this universe. Glory!

Knowing and accepting these facts shifts us into a new paradigm and a new perspective about some things. A new concept about our lives here in the earth realm. We can no longer just limit ourselves to the formula of: get an education, get a good job, get married, have babies. No longer can we allow the thinking of some, that the unborn are simply inconveniences, dispensable and disposable. We must come to realize that each one of these **lives** is a living soul that contains some of the very DNA of God the Father. A True and Living God. A living soul that will live as long as God lives…and He is the beginning and the end (Rev. 1:8). He never dies. He lives and we live throughout eternity. We live eternally with Him…by accepting His son Jesus Christ…or eternally apart from Him…by rejecting Jesus Christ (a living hell, eternal damnation, Rev. 21:8). Souls are **eternal**. Souls are from the breath and Life of God the Father. His DNA. And DNA is eternal. We can now understand a portion of our role as guardians of these souls that we partner with the Father in bringing forth.

What a much broader and more beautiful panorama of marriage we now entertain. After receiving such a divine illumination, young ladies are able to better understand why it's so important to keep themselves and be rightly joined to the right life's partner for them (to minimize bringing forth bruised and tainted fruit). With this revelation of truth they begin to comprehend that their reproductive system is in actuality the gateway to eternity for souls that the lord would lend unto them. Souls that always have and always will belong to God. "All souls are mine saith the Lord", (Ez. 18:4).

Young men will realign their thinking process also. It should become clearer to them that their **seed** is something precious and valuable. It's not to be indiscriminately wasted and misused but it's something made by God himself containing part of the essence of Him and carrying a portion of His life force or DNA. The DNA (Divine Nature Activation) of God the Father is present in the seed of man. The beginning of life. Within man's seed there is life...or lives that will live out their duration on the earth and then spend eternity somewhere. Eternal life. More abundantly in the bosom of God…or eternal damnation; apart from the Father. Where there is weeping and gnashing of teeth (Matt. 8:12). God feels so strongly about His Life source and DNA that He once took a man's earthly life because he spilled his seed onto the ground rather than responding to the purpose and plan of God in continuing the posterity within the earth (Gen. 38:9).

Let us move on to the beautiful type of the Blood Covenant found in the earth realm's marriage relationship. A type that Christ likens to being similar to that of His relationship to His Church. The Body of Christ. Becoming "one" with His Body.

We've discussed the fact that a woman's womb can be considered the **gateway to eternity** for souls that God allows her to carry and nurture and bring forth into the earth. Let's look a little more closely at some of the aspects of this process.

According to my High School Biology instructor, women are born with a thin veil or curtain covering most of the vaginal canal. This wall of membrane is called the Hymen. The **life** canal is veiled by a thin membrane of fleshly tissue that prevents anything foreign from entering as long as it is intact. In order for reproduction to take place, Father God engineered it so that the seed from a male must travel upward through the vaginal canal; through the uterus and into the fallopian tube where it joins with the egg of the woman. When man's seed, or sperm, unites with the woman's egg, fertilization begins. Life starts. The DNA of God that has been passed down from generation to generation since the creation of Adam, once again initiates a **life process**. Conception! Everything is already encoded into that microscopic seed/egg unit to produce another complete human being over a period of time.

I find it interesting that throughout childhood and puberty, as long as a woman remains a virgin this veil of flesh guards and protects this inner sanctum where conception of life takes place. We must note however that modern young women sometimes tear this wall of flesh in various other ways (sports, bike riding, injury, etc.).

On the wedding night, when the marriage is consummated with sexual intercourse, (assuming that both partners are virgins – which **was** and **still is** God's original plan) the man (soon to be king and priest – see my book "Fortifying

Family Fabric"), breaks or rends the veil of partition. There is a shedding of innocent blood. The man releases his seed, and his seed and the blood mingle together initiating a Blood Covenant or Contract between **this** man and **this** woman. Then his seed and her egg unite and become one flesh and a brand new "mini kingdom", or a new family comes into being to help repopulate the earth. Launched with a type of Blood Covenant.

I believe that this is why there is such a significance placed upon the "firstborn" or "first fruits" of a man or family. This is the fruit of the womb (earth) that the father's blessing is handed down to. In one sense, the eldest child was the heir to everything the father possessed because he was the "covenant child". In Old Testament times this first-born son would sometimes be held up to God at birth and the woman would proclaim, "I have received a man child from the Lord". A man that can continue to obey the commands of the Father to be fruitful and multiply. To replenish and subdue the earth.

Also if we study the Old Testament we find another interesting piece of information. On the wedding day or "honeymoon" night, the older women of the family would place white linen on the marriage bed before the couple entered the bride chamber. The next morning the linen would be inspected and if there was no "shedding of blood" or "token of marriage" the groom or the groom's family were permitted to declare the marriage null and void. The community would not recognize the marriage. Harsh, but principle driven (Deut. 22:16-19). These bedclothes, or "tokens of marriage", would be kept by the brides family in trust.

Modern day statisticians and researchers have discovered some amazing facts recently about marriage and divorce. They learned that men and women who marry while they are both still virgins have only a less than 1% chance of ever being divorced. God knew that already. Perhaps Blood Covenants are a much more powerful component of our lives today than we have realized. The DNA of God – through life that is in the blood – contains a dynamic covenant making ability.

Allow me to share with you some inspiring and contemplative parallels between what we've been discussing here and the relationship between Christ and His Church as recorded in the New Testament.

1. Upon Christ's death upon the cross the veil in the temple that separated the Holy place from the Holy of Holies was rent in two (Luke 23:45, Matt. 27:51). He shed His Blood. The veil was torn in two. Beyond that veil was the very Place of the Father. The place that all spiritual life emanated from. Now **new** life, souls, could come forth in the spirit realm. "New Birth" could now take place, Jesus himself being the "firstborn" (Rom. 8:29). When He shed His Blood the veil was rent, giving us **access** to the Kingdom of the Father. Giving is **Divine** Nature Ability. **Divine Nature Attributes. Divine Nature** Activation. **Divine Nature** Access. **Divine Nature** Affection.

2. He then went and sprinkled His Blood upon the Mercy Seat and the furnishings in the Glory realm (Heb. 8, 9). Blood and Seed. His Seed. His Blood. His Church. Blood bought and born with an incorruptible seed. That seed remains in us as long as we receive it by faith and walk obediently and humbly before Him.

3. And now we the Church of Jesus Christ will be part of the "Bride of Christ", that Holy City, New Jerusalem. Coming down from Heaven above (Rev. 3:12, Rev. 21:2). We have a new will and testament written in His Blood. Amen.

Dear reader I implore you today, if you have not accepted Jesus Christ into your **heart** do it **right now**. Ask Him to forgive you of your sins. He will. Confess His name with your mouth. Ask Him to come into your life today. He will. Today is the day of your salvation. Now begin to thank Him for what He has done. Thank you Jesus. (Rom. 10:9, 10)...Today is the first day of the rest of your life!

In the previous paragraphs we were speaking about the natural realm blood covenant that takes place within human marriage. One of the modern day problems that arise is the fact that in today's society, virginity is becoming less and less commonplace. So what is the remedy for thousands of men and women who have a come into the Family of God in these last few generations? Or the precious people of God who are involved in their second or third marriage?

"Wherefore if any man (or woman) be **in Christ**, he (or she) is a "**new Creation**". Old things are passed away; behold they are become **new** (II Cor. 15:17). I believe that once we are born again, (begotten from above), by the water, the Spirit and the Blood, a restoration takes place in the Spirit realm. Not a restoration that can always be seen with the natural eye, but a restoration nonetheless. For those believers who may have lost their virginity while living in the kingdom of darkness, once they have been **translated** into this marvelous Kingdom of Christ- the Kingdom of Light – with that **translation** comes a new right and a new authority to decree and establish covenants (Matt. 18:18-18). Every Spirit-filled, blood bought believer has the God given right an privilege to enter into a spiritual "blood covenant" with their husband or wife based upon what Jesus has already done in the heavenlies (I John 1:7, rev. 1:5, I John 3:2-3, Col. 1:20-23).

Regardless of past relationships, discretions or circumstances you and your spouse can and should live in a covenant relationship with one another. However it is up to each individual to **proclaim** and **decree** such things. It is by faith in His finished work and the DNA of God that indwells the believer. We must speak and appropriate the covenant together in agreement with our spouses (Pr. 18:21, Matt. 12:34).

Men and women, who have lived promiscuous or immoral lives before meeting Christ, become as pure and clean as snow, once they have been washed in the Blood of the Lamb. Cleansed by His Blood (DNA). Restored by His Blood. Redeemed by His Blood. Their **new names** are written in the Lamb's Book of Life, and they are seated with Christ already in heavenly places. His Blood also purges our consciences from the guilt and the shame of our past lives, (Heb. 9:14), and gives us the assurance that we have become "righteous" in God's sight because of the righteousness of Christ.

As a matter of fact, to those who believe in the one and only true God, He will give double honor for their shame, (Mary Magdelene, Rahab, Ethiopian eunuch). You can have the blessed assurance that all of your sins have been washed away, never to be brought up again by God, once the power of His Blood has touched your life.

If you've believed on Jesus, and He and the Father have come to live in you and dwell with you, you have the DNA of God in your life. Divine Nature Ability. Divine Nature Attributes and Divine Nature Access. You now enjoy the benefits of an eternal Blood Covenant. That means you are living under the "commanded blessings" of God. You are now a family member in the family of God. Heirs and joint heirs with Jesus Christ You are legally and morally entitled to what he has left for you in His will and testament. You are an heir. You and I are the testees. He is the testator. We don't have to wait until **we** leave the earth realm to inherit the contents of the will...When the testator, Jesus Christ – God's begotten Son – passed from this life (earth realm) to **His** life, Kingdom realm, that's when all the provisions an contents of the will became the rightful property of the heirs.

The same commanded blessings that rested upon Noah and Abraham and Jacob rests upon our lives by faith in His Blood (DNA). They received the promise by faith in the blood sacrifice. We continue to receive the benefits of that blessing by faith in the eternal Blood of the ultimate sacrifice, Jesus Christ...the Lamb of God, slain from **foundation of the world**!

We can walk under that blessing as long as His seed or DNA remains in us. That incorruptible seed. His Holy seed.

As long as we remain in His Word and in His Spirit, we too can **know** that His hand of **favor** is upon us. What a marvelous and exciting life is available to all who will take up their cross an follow the Lamb of God wither so ever he goes. Amen.

God's purpose for your life is unalterable. His destiny for your life is unpreventable. He knew you before you were born, and He has a design for your life (Jer. 1:5). The enemy cannot twist that design if you will stand firm in your faith in God. As a child of God you are elected for greatness even before the world began (Eph. 1:3-4). God put the life of His Son on the line from the foundation of the world to guarantee you a place in His divine plan (Rev. 13:8). By that plan He predestined you to be adopted as His son (Eph. 1:5). It is His decision. It is the sovereign expression of His mercy (Rom. 9:16). There is nothing anybody can do about that.

The mechanism for natural life is in the blood...
The machinery for natural life is in the blood...
The encoding for natural life is in the blood...

The mechanism for spiritual life is in God's DNA…

The machinery for spiritual life is in God's DNA…

The encoding for spiritual life is in God's DNA…

1-866-381-2665

Printed in the United States
68178LVS00002B/16

9 781591 607557